T0197535

Lola

the Chihuahua that
Wanted to Be a Goat!

Written By: Deborah Soffer Tarbell   Illustrated By: Stacy Gertis

To order additional copies of this book, contact:
Xlibris
844-714-8691
www.Xlibris.com
Orders@Xlibris.com

ISBN: Softcover   978-1-6698-5569-9
        Hardcover   978-1-6698-5568-2
        EBook   978-1-6698-5567-5

Library of Congress Control Number: 2022921246

Print information available on the last page

Rev. date: 11/25/2022

This book is dedicated to my daughter Brooke. I love you with all of my heart and soul. Without you and Lola Cindy Lou Who, this book would never have been written.

Lola was a chihuahua, but she wanted to be a goat. This happened the day our goats Chance and Flower arrived. Lola was in love!

Before we got our goats, Lola was content to eat her dog food and her favorite snacks of carrots and toast crusts.

But once Chance and Flower arrived
Lola would only eat goat grain!

Lola loved goat grain so much she would sneak out of the house to eat grain with the goats.

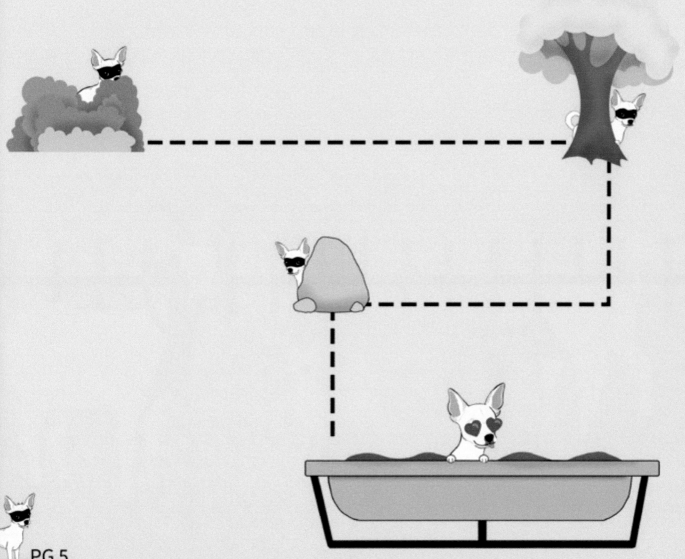

Not only did Lola love goat grain, but she would also blissfully graze on the lush, green grass with Chance and Flower all day.

Lola also loved basking in the warm sun
alongside Chance and Flower.

As the weeks passed by,
Brooke and I started noticing
subtle changes in Lola.
As we were petting her one
day, we noticed tiny little
bumps behind her ears!

Lola was also having a hard time walking and balancing herself. When we looked closer, we noticed that her delicate chichi paws were taking the shape of cloven hooves.
Just like goats!

But by watching the goats, Lola regained her footing and was running and jumping, kicking her back legs sideways into the air!

The goats loved playing with Lola. They were spending the long summer days together and were accepting Lola as one of their own. This was good.... and not so good.

You see, when goats play, they ram into each other with their horns! But Lola was so little they would butt her into the air, and she would land with a thud on her little chichi butt. Poor Lola!

Brooke and I came up with an idea to put pillows on Lola's butt to cushion her falls. This worked well because Lola was also developing a thick coat of fur...just like the goats! Now she could run and play without her little butt being bruised.

Although Lola seemed very happy and healthy, we decided to take her to the veterinarian for a checkup.

The vet couldn't find a reason to explain the changes in Lola. Aside from the physical changes she was experiencing, Lola was happy, healthy and thriving.

So, we brought Lola back home and reunited her with Chance and Flower. They were so happy to see one another!

A few more weeks passed, and we noticed Lola was losing her teeth! We would find tiny little pearls scattered throughout the house!

This was odd, because just like goats she had bottom teeth, but very few on top!

Now Brooke and I were very confused! We called and made an appointment to see the vet again when the weekend was over.

The next day was a beautiful Saturday afternoon.
Brooke and I were sitting outside eating popsicles. Which
was one of our favorite things to do in the summer.

Suddenly, we heard a flurry of noise! As Brooke and I turned to look, we spied Lola... or what used to be Lola! She was standing on tiny little hooves. She had a thick, course coat and tiny little horns has sprouted atop her head. She had a toothless grin and was bleating "Ma Ma"

We burst out laughing because she was the tiniest, cutest little goat we had ever seen! Although she was not the Lola we had known and loved before her strange metamorphosis, we loved her more because she was still our Lola!

Printed in the United States
by Baker & Taylor Publisher Services